Original Korean text by Ji-seul Hahm
Illustrations by David Lupton
Korean edition © Yeowon Media Co., Ltd.

This English edition published by big & SMALL in 2016
by arrangement with Yeowon Media Co., Ltd.
English text edited by Joy Cowley
English edition © big & SMALL 2016

Distributed in the United States and Canada by
Lerner Publishing Group, Inc.
241 First Avenue North
Minneapolis, MN 55401 U.S.A.
www.lernerbooks.com

5-16
√E Hah

ISBN: 978-1-925247-39-8

Printed in Korea

Prokofiev's

Peter and
the Wolf

Retold by Ji-seul Hahm   Illustrated by David Lupton
Edited by Joy Cowley

Peter and his grandfather live in a house in a forest. Grandfather has told Peter not to go out on his own just in case he meets a big, scary wolf.
When Peter ignores his grandfather's advice and goes out anyway, what will happen?

Here are the characters in the story. Each one is represented by the musical instrument next to it.

Little Bird
flute

Cat
clarinet

Grey Wolf
French horn

Duck
oboe

Grandfather
bassoon

Hunters
timpani and bass drum

Peter
string instruments

One day, very early in the morning,
Peter woke up before his grandfather.
He went out, opened the garden gate
and stepped into the meadow,
leaving the garden gate open.

A little bird flew to the top of a big tree.
"What a peaceful morning this is!" it sang.
It chirped and chirped, and its song grew louder.

The duck was pleased to see the gate open.
"Oh good! I can take a swim in the pond!"
It waddled down to the pond in the meadow.

The little bird flew down to the pond
and fluttered toward the duck.
"What kind of bird cannot fly?" it teased.

The duck got angry and quacked,
"What kind of bird cannot swim?"

The teasing went on and on.

A cat crawled out from under a bush,
and silently sneaked closer to the pond.
"The duck and the bird are busy arguing.
I can catch them both, and eat them!"

Peter's eyes nearly popped out
when he saw what was about to happen.

Peter shouted, "Bird! Duck! Be careful!"

The little bird quickly flew back to the tree.
The duck swam to the middle of the pond
and quacked noisily at the cat.

The cat looked up at the bird in the tree.
"If I climb the tree,
the silly little thing will fly away."

Grandfather was angry to see Peter in the meadow.
He grabbed him by the hand and pulled him along.
"I've told you it's dangerous to go out on your own.
What would you do if a wolf came along?"
He took Peter back inside, and locked the gate.

Not long after, a shadow came out of the forest.
It was a big grey wolf, strolling toward the pond.
When the cat saw the wolf, it shot up a tree,
but the duck was so surprised that it didn't think.
It quacked and jumped right out of the pond.

The wolf ran after the frightened duck.
Closer and closer!
The duck could not run fast enough.
The wolf got so close that it caught the duck
with a swipe of its paw.
Then it swallowed the duck in one gulp.

Peter watched all this from the garden gate.
He saw the cat sitting on a tree branch
and the little bird perched in another tree.
The wolf drooled as it walked
around and around, looking at the bird.

Peter saw all of this, but he wasn't scared.

Peter ran to the cellar and got some strong rope.
He climbed onto the wall and from there
he jumped into the branches of the tree.
He whispered to the bird,
"Little bird, fly around above the wolf's head.
Stay out of reach. Don't let it catch you."

The little bird flew low and teased the wolf.
"Bad wolf! Catch me if you can!"

The wolf got angry and jumped up,
swinging its front paws wildly.
But the little bird was too quick.

Peter made a lasso with the rope.
Carefully, he dropped the lasso down.
When it looped over the wolf's tail,
he pulled the rope with all his strength.

The surprised wolf thrashed around,
but the rope was so tight around its tail,
it could do nothing.
Peter tied the rope to the tree.

At that moment, hunters came out of the forest.
They saw the wolf and aimed their guns.

"Don't shoot!" Peter called from the wall.
"We've already caught the wolf.
Please help us take it to the zoo."

They paraded to the zoo.
Peter marched at the front,
and behind him the hunters
carried the wolf, tied with rope.

Grandfather and the cat followed.
Grandfather shook his head at Peter.
"What would have happened to you
if you hadn't caught the wolf?"

The little bird flew above them.
"*Chirp! Chirp!* Peter and I are brave.
We caught the wolf together."

"Quack! Quack!"
Can you hear something?
Yes, it's the sound of the duck.
The wolf swallowed it whole, and now
it is quacking inside the wolf's stomach!

♪: Let's Learn About **Peter and the Wolf**

🐦 Sergei Prokofiev

Born: 23 April 1891
Died: 5 March 1953
Place of birth: Sontsovka (now Krasne) in Eastern Ukraine
Biography: A Russian composer, pianist, and conductor, Prokofiev showed his remarkable musical ability at the age of five when he composed his first piano piece. When he was thirteen, he entered the Saint Petersburg Conservatory and studied piano, composition, and conducting techniques. As a composer, he created modern music which was considered well ahead of its time. In 1918, Prokofiev left Russia, living in the United States, Germany, and France, and working as a composer, pianist, and conductor. In 1936, he returned to Russia with his family. It was in the days when Stalin ruled Russia, and artistic expression and performance were tightly controlled. So Prokofiev composed film music, ballets, and music for children as these things were less regulated. He died suddenly in 1953. His most celebrated works were the operas *The Love for Three Oranges* and *War and Peace*, the film music *Lieutenant Kijé*, the ballet *Romeo and Juliet*, and the children's fable *Peter and the Wolf*. He is regarded as one of the major composers of the twentieth century.

Saint Petersburg Conservatory

Prokofiev featured on a special stamp in 1991

The Story of **Peter and the Wolf**

Both the music and words for *Peter and the Wolf* were
written by Prokofiev in 1936. It is a children's story, told
by a narrator and accompanied by an orchestra.
Prokofiev composed it after the Central Children's
Theater in Moscow asked him to write a symphony for
children, and it introduces musical instruments to children
through storytelling. *Peter and the Wolf* gives each character
a particular instrument and a musical theme: the cat has
the clarinet, the bird has the flute, the duck has the oboe,
Peter's grandfather has the bassoon, the hunters have the
drums, Peter has string instruments, and the wolf has
French horns. Each instrument plays its theme melody,
and the narrator tells the story along with the music.

Prokofiev and his children

♫ Let's Find Out About the Music

The characters in the story are each represented by different musical instruments.

Wolf

Three French horns take the role of the wolf. Their low, harmonious notes capture the tone of the scary wolf.

Peter's Grandfather

The bassoon takes the grandfather's role. It produces the lowest sound of all woodwind instruments, and it perfectly describes the gruff personality of Peter's grandfather.

Duck

The duck is played by the oboe. The main theme represents the duck which is gently gliding over the water, and this is played alongside Peter's theme when he is marching.

Hunters

The hunters are played by the timpani (a type of drum) and a bass drum. These drums help to capture the sound of their gunshots.

Cat

The clarinet takes the role of the cat. Its low, steady, smooth sound provides the image of the cat as it chases after the bird.

Bird

The bird is played by the flute. The high, light sound of the flute is perfect for describing the bird.

Peter

The strings express Peter's braveness. The strings are made up of a first and second violin, a viola, a cello, and a double bass.

Let's Discover the Instruments

Let's find out more about the instruments played in *Peter and the Wolf*.

 String Orchestra

A string orchestra is a musical group made up of instruments only from the string family. These instruments are the violin, the viola, the cello, and the double bass. The strings produce a rich, harmonious sound. One instrument plays the main melody and is accompanied by the other instruments.

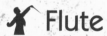 Flute

The flute is popular woodwind instrument with a clear, transparent sound. This is produced by blowing air into the mouthpiece. A flute player changes the pitch of the sound by opening and closing holes in the body of the instrument. In early days, flutes were wooden, but today they are made of silver, gold, and even platinum.

Oboe

The oboe is a woodwind instrument with a double reed. These are cane reeds, and they have a big effect on the sound of the instrument. The oboe has a low and gentle sound, and usually orchestras tune to this.

Clarinet

The clarinet has a single reed and a straight body. Because of its beautiful tone and wide ranging sound, it's an important woodwind instrument. Today, the clarinet is commonly used in classical music, military marching bands, and jazz bands.

Bassoon

The bassoon has the longest body of all woodwind instruments and it produces the lowest, deepest sound. A bassoonist produces the sound by blowing air into the reed which is fitted to a metal "crook" (a piece of tube). Because of its sound, which often expresses funny, silly moods, the bassoon has been nicknamed the "clown of the orchestra."

Horn

As you might guess from the name, originally horns came from animals. People blew into them to create sounds. Later they were made from metal, so the horn is classed as a brass instrument. A horn player controls the pitch by pressing the valves with their left hand, and putting their right hand inside the bell to change the style and mood of the sound.

Timpani

Timpani, or kettledrums, are part of the percussion family. They are played by striking the heads, made of calfskin or plastic, with timpani sticks. There is a pedal, connected to tension screws, which is used to change the pitch of the instrument. The powerful booming sounds of the timpani help build atmosphere in a climax.

Bass Drum

The bass drum is a large drum which produces a low, booming sound. Both ends of the drum are covered with heads made of calfskin or plastic, and it is played by striking these heads with a mallet. Bass drums are made in different sizes, and the mallet is usually wooden and wrapped in felt.

E Hah
Hahm, Ji-seul,
Prokofiev's Peter and the
wolf